Paperback ISBN: 978-1-63731-990-1   Hardcover ISBN: 978-1-63731-991-8

Copyright © SEL Enterprise
Printed 2024 - All rights Reserved

We reserve all rights to copyright, illustrations, and design.

November was a **curious** boy
With a scarf wrapped around his neck.
He'd solve a puzzle in no time flat.
He always kept things in check.

He called his pal, Mr. Turkey.
"Hey, did you catch a clue?
My calendar's been **GOBBLED** up,
What am I gonna do?"

Mr. Turkey flapped his wings and sighed,
"The wind was **WILD** last night.
It tossed those numbers all around
Till they were out of sight."

November **THOUGHT** and **SCRATCHED** his head,
"That wind was strong, no doubt,
But wind doesn't gobble up the dates—
Something else is about."

"**AHA**!" November snapped his fingers,
"The Calendar Squirrel's near!
He's taken all my favorite dates,
But now it's all so clear!"

He set a trap with nuts and seeds,
And placed them near each date
With pumpkins, turkeys, and autumn leaves,
He **HOPED** it wasn't too late.

He hid behind a bale of hay,
And waited, heart a-thump.
The night was **CRISP**, the moon was **HIGH**.
His heart was set to jump.

Then **SUDDENLY**, the Squirrel appeared.
He giggled, quick and sly.
He reached to nab another date,
But fell for his clever lie!

From then on, all their days
Were full of **CHEER**.
The dates stayed put, the fun began
With Thanksgiving drawing near.

Now November checks his calendar
With Squirrel by his side.
They mark the days, plan the **FUN**,
And take it all in stride.

CRAFT ACTIVITY: ACORN NECKLACES

Let's get crafty with a charm,
Make an acorn necklace sweet,
It's simple, fun, and stylish too,
A fall accessory treat!

You'll Need:

* ACORNS (WITH CAPS STILL ATTACHED)
* TWINE, YARN, OR A THIN LEATHER CORD (FOR THE NECKLACE)
* SMALL SCREW EYE HOOKS (AVAILABLE AT CRAFT STORES)
* PLIERS (FOR SCREWING IN THE HOOKS)
* OPTIONAL: BEADS, CHARMS, OR PAINT FOR DECORATION

Instructions:

1. Collect Your Acorns:
- Gather acorns from outside, making sure the caps are still attached. You can also buy them at a craft store if needed.
- Clean the acorns by wiping them with a damp cloth to remove any dirt.

2. Prepare the Acorns:
- Use small pliers to carefully screw a tiny eye hook into the top of each acorn, where the cap meets the nut. Twist gently but firmly until the hook is secure. **Tip: If the acorns are tough to screw into, you can gently start the hole with a push pin or small drill.

3. CUT THE NECKLACE CORD:
- Cut a piece of twine, yarn, or leather cord long enough to fit over your head (about 24-28 inches, depending on your preference).
- String the acorn through the eye hook so it dangles like a charm.

4. ADD DECORATIVE ELEMENTS (OPTIONAL):
- If you'd like to add some extra flair, slide beads or charms onto the cord alongside the acorn.
- You can also paint the acorn caps or nuts in fall colors for a more personalized look.

5. TIE THE NECKLACE:
- Tie the ends of the cord together with a secure knot, creating a loop for your necklace.
- Make sure the knot is tight and the length of the necklace is comfortable to wear.

6. WEAR AND ENJOY!:
- Slip the necklace over your head and show off your new fall-inspired accessory!
- You can make matching sets for friends or family for a fun fall-themed gift.

FALL RECIPE: CRANBERRY CORNBREAD MUFFINS

Whip up a treat that's sweet and tart,
With cranberry flavor bright,
These muffins are the perfect side,
To warm up any night!

YOU'LL NEED:

* 1 CUP CORNMEAL
* 1 CUP ALL-PURPOSE FLOUR
* 1/4 CUP SUGAR
* 1 TABLESPOON BAKING POWDER
* 1/2 TEASPOON SALT
* 1/2 TEASPOON CINNAMON (OPTIONAL, FOR A FALL FLAVOR TWIST)
* 1 CUP MILK (OR BUTTERMILK FOR EXTRA RICHNESS)
* 1/4 CUP MELTED BUTTER (OR VEGETABLE OIL)
* 1 LARGE EGG
* 1 CUP FRESH OR FROZEN CRANBERRIES (CHOPPED IN HALF)
* 1/4 CUP HONEY (FOR EXTRA SWEETNESS)
* 1 TEASPOON VANILLA EXTRACT (OPTIONAL)
* ZEST OF 1 ORANGE (OPTIONAL, FOR EXTRA CITRUS FLAVOR)

INSTRUCTIONS:

1. PREHEAT THE OVEN:

- Preheat your oven to 400°F (200°C) and grease a muffin tin or line it with paper liners.

INSTRUCTIONS (CONT.):

2. MIX THE DRY INGREDIENTS:
- In a large mixing bowl, combine the cornmeal, flour, sugar, baking powder, salt, and cinnamon (if using). Stir well to blend.

3. COMBINE WET INGREDIENTS:
- In a separate bowl, whisk together the milk, melted butter, egg, honey, and vanilla extract (if using) until smooth.

4. COMBINE WET AND DRY INGREDIENTS:
- Pour the wet ingredients into the dry ingredients. Stir gently until just combined. Be careful not to overmix.
- Fold in the cranberries and orange zest (if using) to add bursts of tartness and flavor.

5. FILL THE MUFFIN TIN:
- Spoon the batter into the prepared muffin tin, filling each cup about 2/3 full.

6. BAKE THE MUFFINS:
- Bake for 15-18 minutes or until the tops are golden and a toothpick inserted into the center of a muffin comes out clean.

7. BAKE THE MUFFINS:
- Let the muffins cool in the tin for 5 minutes, then transfer them to a wire rack to cool completely.
- Serve warm with butter or honey for an extra treat, or enjoy them as a side with dinner.